THE GIA[NT]
Who Wanted Company

BY LEE PRIESTLY
ILLUSTRATED BY DENNIS HOCKERMAN

For Brianna, Mace, and Sarah,
who helped.

A GOLDEN BOOK, New York
Western Publishing Company, Inc.
Racine, Wisconsin 53404

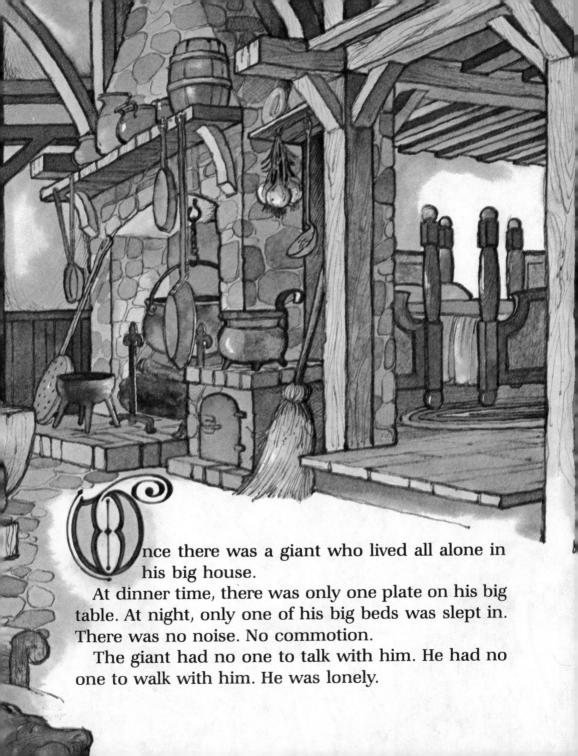

Once there was a giant who lived all alone in his big house.

At dinner time, there was only one plate on his big table. At night, only one of his big beds was slept in. There was no noise. No commotion.

The giant had no one to talk with him. He had no one to walk with him. He was lonely.

"I'd like some company," the giant said to himself. "I'll go far and near, and I'll invite my friends to come visit me."

So he went far to invite his giant friends. "I'd like some company," the giant said to them. "Could you stop by to see me someday?"

"We'll be glad to come," said his giant friends. "See you soon!"

Next the giant went near to invite his smaller friends. He invited horses and cows and dogs and cats, kittens and goats and llamas and bats, and ants and doves.

"I'd like some company," the giant said to them all. "Could you stop by to see me someday?"

"We'll be glad to come," said his smaller friends. "See you soon!"

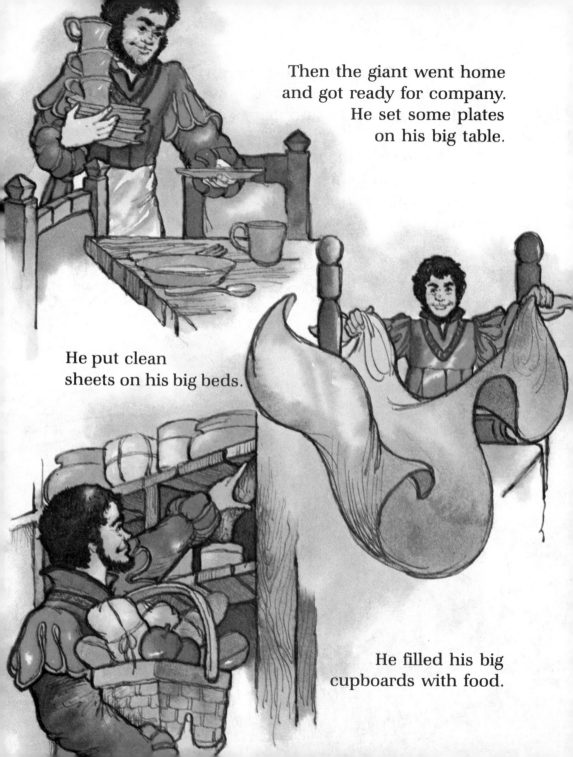

Then the giant went home
and got ready for company.
He set some plates
on his big table.

He put clean
sheets on his big beds.

He filled his big
cupboards with food.

When everything was ready, the giant sat down to wait for visitors. He wondered who would come first—giant friends or smaller friends.

Soon he heard knocking. Someone was knocking at his big front door! The giant hurried to open it, and—

He saw *all* his giant friends! *All* his smaller friends! All the company, from far and near, had come at once!

There was noise in the giant's house then. He had so much company to talk with!

The giants shouted, the horses neighed, the cows mooed, the dogs barked, the cats meowed, the kittens mewed, the goats bleated, the llamas made whatever kind of noise llamas make, the bats squeaked, the ants chirred, and the doves cooed.

In all that noise, the giant couldn't understand a single word anyone said.

There was commotion in the giant's house then. He had so much company to walk with!

The giants strode, the horses cantered, the cows plodded, the dogs trotted, the cats prowled, the kittens scampered, the goats ambled, the llamas moved in whatever way llamas move, the bats swooped, the ants scattered, and the doves flew.

In all that commotion, the giant didn't dare to set a foot down flat for fear of stepping on a friend.

The giant had so much company to feed!
He seated all his giant friends around his big table.
They ate the toast and the roast, the ham and the
jam—and everything else from the cupboards, too.

He brought in hay from the stables for the horses.

He gathered grass from the pasture for the cows.

He found bones from the meat for the dogs.

"But I've still got so much company left over!" said the giant.

So...
the cats looked for scraps,
the kittens ate the lickin's
   (scraped from the cooking pots),
the goats chose oats,
the llamas ate whatever llamas eat,
the bats searched for this-and-thats,
the ants did a sugar bowl dance,
and the doves—*what* could he feed
   the doves?

Then the doves, who
were always polite, cooed
and cooed. "Never mind,
Giant. We aren't hungry."
   But the giant was.
And he had to stay hungry,
for there was nothing left
for him to eat.

The giant had so much company to spend the night!

His giant friends slept in the giant beds. The horses slept in the chairs, the cows slept on the sofas, and the dogs slept on the footstools.

"But I've still got so much company left over!" said the giant.

So. . .
he put the cats to bed on the mats,
the kittens in his mittens,
the goats in his coats,
the llamas in his pajamas. . .

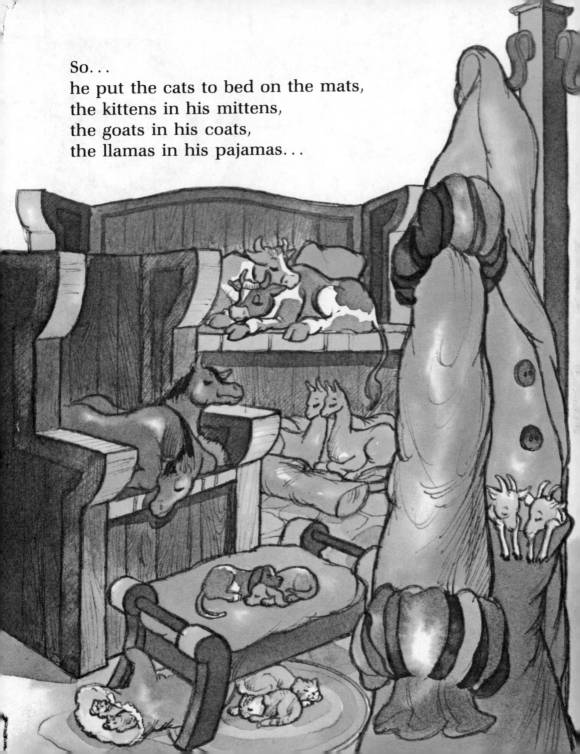

the bats in his hats,
the ants on his plants,
and the doves in his gloves.

Then the tired giant tried to sleep leaning against a table leg.

The next morning, all the company woke early. They hadn't slept very well in their strange beds.

They were hungry, too, but there was nothing for breakfast. They had eaten everything the night before.

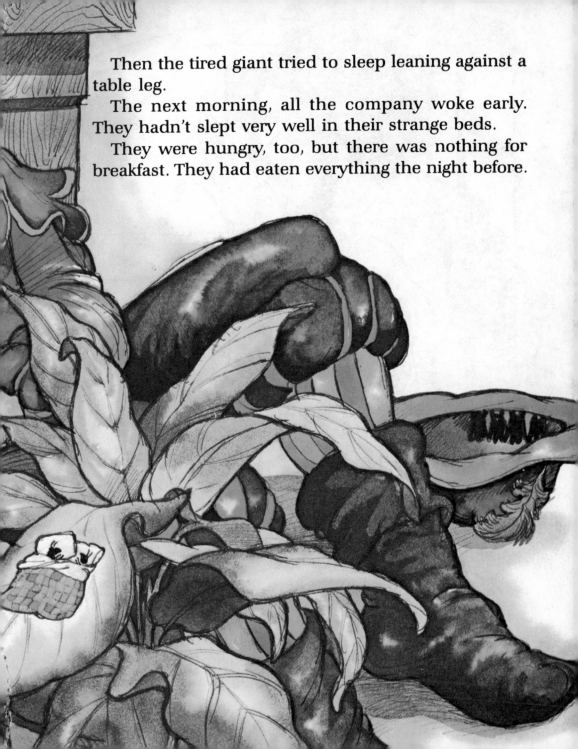

So all the company, great and small, told the giant
they'd had a nice time, but they had to go home now.
The giant hurried to open his big front door.

"Good-bye, good-bye," said the sleepy, hungry giant.
"Come again sometime—but, please, not all at once!
I'll tell you when!"